D1202004

THE MIRROR PLANET

Published by Creative Education, Inc., 123 South Broad Street, Mankato,
Minnesota 56001. Copyright© 1978 by Creative Education, Inc. International
copyrights reserved in all countries. No part of this book may be reproduced in
any form without permission from the publisher. Printed in the United States.
Distributed by Children's Press, 1224 West Van Buren Street, Chicago, Illinois 60607.

Library of Congress Cataloging in Publication Data

Bunting, Anne Eve.
  The mirror planet.

  SUMMARY: On a televiewer, Andy discovers another self who can tell him
what will happen up to eight days in the future. The possibilities seem exciting
until disaster strikes.
  [1. Science fiction] I. Title.
PZ7.B91527Mi   [Fic]   78-4541
ISBN 0-87191-628-2

THE MIRROR PLANET

Written by Eve Bunting
Illustrated by Don Hendricks

Creative Education
Childrens Press

Andy walked across the schoolyard with Gilbert. It was hot and the sky was a cloudless blue. Andy searched overhead for the hint of a cloud, but there wasn't one in sight. Of course it wasn't going to rain. Just because he and his mirrored self were breaking some space-time law.

"How's it going, Andy?" someone called.

Troy Hamill flashed his white grin in their direction. "What's happening, Andy?"

Andy nodded and tried to act as if it were old stuff to him, having all the guys in school know his name. Being chunky, and bad at sports and a brain weren't exactly the things that made kids notice you in Macmillan High. Nobody had noticed him before. Not until IT happened.

Gilbert looked at him sideways. "I'm surprised you still walk with me. I mean, a hot shot like you!"

"Don't be dumb," Andy said. "You're my friend. Am I the kind of guy who would ditch a friend just because I've become...." He searched for words. "Just because I've become special?" he finished weakly.

Gilbert shrugged. "I don't know what kind of a guy you are anymore. And anyway, I always thought you *were* special."

"Sure!"

Someone was running across the cement behind them and he heard his name called. He turned around. It was Jim Harrison who was a senior and played short stop on the Varsity baseball team.

"Wait up, Andy." Jim fell into step beside them. Andy couldn't help noticing that he didn't bother to speak to Gilbert who was chunky too, and bad at sports, and as much of a brain as Andy. Two peas in a pod, Andy thought. No wonder we're friends.

"Listen, Andy." Jim Harrison walked with his hands in his pockets and his head down.

2

"I hear you've been doing some pretty neat things. I'm really impressed. Hey, can I ask you something?"

"Here it comes," Gilbert muttered.

"You know about the game tomorrow night against Hoover?" Jim asked.

Andy nodded.

"Do you know yet who's going to win?"

"That's not the way it works," Andy said. "I mean, I don't just know things. I have to concentrate. It takes time."

"Oh yeah?" Jim's sharp little eyes met his for a second and then darted away. "Well, why don't you think about it for a while and then call me at home. My number's in the book."

"Well...." Andy hesitated. He almost said, "Maybe it will rain." But Jim would think he was crazy. Who ever heard of rain in Southern California in June? He glanced nervously at the sky and decided to say nothing.

Jim grabbed Andy's arm. "I'm kind of nervous about this game. I mean, I'm going to have trouble sleeping and stuff. Short stop's a pretty important position. That's the guy who fields between second base and..."

3

Andy interrupted him. "I know where the short stop plays, for Pete's sake!"

Jim grinned. "Well, if I knew for sure we'd win I'd settle down and quit feeling so jumpy."

"Suppose he tells you you're going to lose?" Gilbert asked.

"Who told you to butt in?" Jim said. He smiled at Andy. "What do you say? Will you phone me when it comes to you?"

"OK."

"Oh, and one more thing, Andy." Jim's eyes swam with sincerity. "I'd appreciate it if you didn't spread the word around. I mean, there are some guys who would have a tough time taking the news either way. They mightn't try so hard in the game."

"Oh, we understand," Gilbert said. He didn't wait till Jim Harrison was out of earshot before he gave a disbelieving snort. "That guy never lost sleep over anything in his life. You know what he's up to, don't you? He'd gamble on how long it takes a spider to spin its web. Tomorrow morning he'll be in the bathroom taking bets on the game, making himself a pile of money. You shouldn't tell him Andy. Honest."

They waited for the streetlight to change.

"You don't know he wants to bet on it," Andy said feebly. He felt Gilbert looking at him and he pretended to be studying his notebook cover.

"Yes I do. And you do too. You just don't want to say no to him or to any of those other goons. You're afraid you'll lose this great new fame or popularity or whatever it is. You make me sick." Gilbert sprinted across the street, though the "Don't Walk" was still flashing.

"Hey," Andy called, but Gilbert didn't even slow down.

Andy waited for the green signal. Who cared about Gilbert anyway? So what if they'd been friends since the third grade? Gilbert was just jealous because Andy had other friends now, besides him. And I almost told him the whole secret, Andy thought. He was glad now that he hadn't. Gilbert was just the kind of goody-good who'd start worrying about the rain thing and about Andy's responsibilities to the world. He

6

was glad nobody knew about the mirror planet except himself. And one other person. And that other person didn't count, because it was really only himself.

It still gave Andy a nervous flick in his stomach each time he thought about it. Though now it wasn't as bad as it had been in the beginning. That first time had been definitely the scariest, creepiest moment of his entire life.

He'd been tinkering with the cosmic televiewer he'd made, bleeping in and out through the static of the other astral bodies when a shadow came on the magnascreen. The shadow was fuzzy, but it was definitely a person. His heart had begun to pound.

Looking back on it since, he'd decided that he'd known right away that something astonishing was happening. But he'd never imagined how astonishing.

When the picture had cleared and settled he found he was looking at himself. He'd even leaned forward and passed his hand in front of his face, expecting to see the mirrored image follow his movements. But the mirror boy, who was Andy Jordan, sat staring, obviously as frightened as he was.

There he was in his own corner-of-the-bedroom lab, sitting at his own work table with the black splotch on it where he'd spilled acid, looking out of the magnascreen at himself. But he was wearing his blue T shirt instead of the white one with the penguin on the pocket that he'd put on this morning. He touched the penguin threads with shaking fingers. What was happening?

The mirror boy spoke first. "Who the heck are you?" And it was Andy's own, gruff, scratchy voice.

"Well, I'm...I'm..." He coughed to cover up his panic. "I'm Andy Jordan."

"How can you be? I'm Andy Jordan."

They'd eyed each other warily, suspecting a trick maybe. At least a trick of their own imaginations. It had taken Andy weeks to accept the reality of it.

I'm not sure I accept it yet, he thought,

jumping the low hedge in front of his house.

He saw at once that his little brother, Briney, was already home. His bike lay on the patch of grass where he'd thrown it. Unlocked as usual, Andy thought. Briney would never learn. Somebody could hop the hedge and pick the bike up and ride off on it. They'd all told Briney that, but did he listen? It wasn't much of a bike. He'd bought it himself with his paper route money. But still.

Andy opened the front door and yelled inside.

"Come out here, Briney, and lock your bike, you dum-dum!"

Nobody answered. Briney must be next door in Jeff's house.

Andy dropped his books on the hall table, went out again and moved the three speed behind a clump of shrubbery. Serve him right!

He put the chain on the front door. That way Briney would have to ring to get in and Andy would have time to blank the magnascreen.

One good thing about having a mom who worked was that a guy could spend as much time as he liked in his bedroom without

9

having her tell him he should go out and get some exercise.

Andrew came on the magna screen as soon as Andy pushed the code letters. They'd decided it would be easier if Andy stayed Andy and the mirror boy became Andrew.

"Andrew's what Mom calls me when she's mad," Andrew had said.

"I know. She's my mom too." Andy didn't like the possessive way Andrew talked about *his* mom. But that was dumb, because, after all, she was Andrew's mom too. How could you be jealous of yourself? It was sure confusing.

Today Andrew's image was sharp and clear.

"I have to ask you something," Andy said.

"Yes. It *is* still raining," Andrew told him.

Andy spoke quickly. "That's not what I was going to ask. It's about the baseball game tomorrow night. The game against Hoover."

"Yeah?"

"Who's going to win it? I mean, who won it?"

"What do you want to know for?"

It drove Andy buggy the way Andrew had to know the details of everything. Then he remembered that Andrew and Andy were the same. He probably did that too. He told Andrew why he wanted to know.

"Finding me here on the mirror planet sure worked out good for you," Andrew said. "Jim Harrison never talks to me."

Andy recognized the tone. He'd already started listing the things that annoyed him most about Andrew, writing them down so he could try to change himself. His list was rat-tail long already. "Are you going to tell me or not?"

"No. I don't know. I never go to ball-games. They're a waste of time."

Andy bit his lip. "Can't you go look it up in the school paper? The scores are listed."

Andrew sighed. "I'll have to find it. Tune back in ten minutes."

"Thanks," Andy said to a screen that was already dark. He got his notebook from his desk and added the two new items to his "Needs Improvement" list. Then he added, "Don't be so superior about baseball just because you aren't

11

interested in it. It sounds nauseating."

He went downstairs to grab some milk and cookies and then he sat at the kitchen table to munch and contemplate again the miracle that had befallen him.

It had taken them a while to figure out that Andrew's world was eight days ahead of Andy's.

"A time gap, way back somewhere at the creation of the universe," Andrew had said.

"Do you think there's another mirror planet that's eight days ahead of you, and another ahead of that?" Andy wondered. It boggled the mind to think about it.

"It's pretty neat for you anyway," Andrew said. "And not so neat for me. I mean, I know what's happened. You can ask me and find out."

Andy agreed. He couldn't believe his good luck. And since then his life had been totally incredible. He, Andy Klutz Jordan had been written up in the school paper. And they'd run his picture next to the one of the Macmillan

Musclemen Rockers. It was a klutzy picture, lifted right out of last year's freshman yearbook. But underneath it said, "Is it Black Magic? E.S.P.? Or does sophomore Andy Jordan use a crystal ball? The soothsayer isn't saying." Then it told how he'd forecast who would win the debating society contest. He'd even predicted the judges' scores. It was after the article that fame hit. Suddenly everybody knew him.

"Are you going to let me in on it?" Gilbert had asked. But something had warned Andy to keep Andrew a secret.

Andrew! He ate the last cookie, drained the milk carton and raced back upstairs. The red light was on.

"Where have you been?" Andrew asked accusingly as soon as he came on the screen. "I bet you were in the kitchen, stuffing yourself as usual."

Andy glared right back. "You should talk! You overeat too." Andrew's mom probably lectured him too about empty calories. It was pretty un-nerving though, having yourself confront

13

yourself like this. It was worse than a conscience. "Did you find the score?" he asked.

"The game was rained out," Andrew said.

"Are you sure?"

"That's what it says here. I told you it's been raining for more than a week here."

Andy stared at what could have been the reflection of his own face. He didn't want to think about what Andrew had said to him a couple of days back. He didn't want to think about the rain.

Andrew was shuffling around in the clutter on his work table.

"Say, how did we do on that English paper?" Andy asked, hoping to take Andrew's

The farmers have lost all their berry crops. There are going to be all kinds of food shortages.

---

mind off rain and other things.

"We got a B plus," Andrew said vaguely.

"Too bad." Andy could see that Andrew wasn't going to be diverted.

"This is what I was looking for." Andrew held a page of newspaper up to the viewer. It was the front of the Sentinel, the paper Briney delivered door to door each evening.

"This is last night's," Andrew said.

"SOUTHERN CALIFORNIA DELUGE," Andy read. "Sacramento River floods its banks." The rest of the print was too small for him to see. "Pretty weird," he said uncomfortably.

Andrew put the paper down. "The farmers have lost all their berry crops. There are going to be all kinds of food shortages. Engineers

15

are on special duty inspecting dams and reservoirs. You know Dopple Dam?"

Andy nodded. "Sure. It's right above us."

"It's supposed to be safe enough though it got jolted back in the earthquake. But Dad's real nervous about it. He says there'd be tons of water if that thing collapsed."

Instinctively Andy looked out of the window toward the hill where the dam crouched, almost expecting to see the giant wave crashing down. But the hill drowsed peacefully in the late afternoon sunshine.

"It says here that the weathermen are baffled," Andrew said. "But we're not baffled, huh, Andy?"

Andy shrugged. "You're only guessing. We don't know for sure."

"We're breaking the space-time continuum. We have to be. Since we're on mirror planets the rule would have to be that what happens on my world has already happened on yours, right? But we're changing the pattern. If the pattern held, then eight days ago I should have been sitting here talking to a guy on a planet eight days ahead of me. Mirrors of mirrors.

What you said at the beginning. Do you see? Or is it too complicated for you?"

"Of course I see. Do you think I'm a dum-dum?" It bugged him that Andrew was talking to him the way he talked to Briney. And of course he understood. He'd suspected it way back, when Andrew first mentioned the strange, heavy rain.

"It's too big a thing to happen," he told Andrew defensively. "A deluge, for Pete's sake. Two guys talking to each other in their own bedrooms, with nobody knowing? Come on! What's that in the scheme of the universe?" He didn't know if he were trying to persuade Andrew, or himself. What if Andrew decided to quit? Then all the excitement would go again. He wouldn't know anything ahead of time. And Jim Harrison and the other hot shots would go back to ignoring him.

"If Earth heated or cooled just a fraction, would it change the scheme of the universe?" Andrew asked.

And do I talk in such a snooty, know-it-all way, Andy wondered. Out loud he said, "Well, I vote we keep right on talking to each

17

other. None of it is our fault."

Andrew's eyes looked right into his. Un-nerving wasn't the word for it. "I knew that's the way you would vote," Andrew said.

Andy felt his face getting warm. Heck, the guy could see right inside his head. Face it, the guy was right inside his head. But then, it worked the other way too. He was right inside Andrew's head. And he knew Andrew didn't want to quit either. Andrew's life was dull. It was the way Andy's had been, before. This contact was the most exciting thing that had ever happened to either of them. It might not be as good for Andrew as for Andy. But it was better than nothing.

"And don't try kidding me either," Andy said softly. "I know you want to keep on too."

There was dislike in Andrew's eyes. Andy disliked him too. How odd, he thought. I've never thought I was too great. But it's pretty bad feeling this way about yourself.

It was a relief to hear the doorbell. Briney always rang like an Avon lady who'd gone out of her head.

"I've got to go," Andy said. "It's Briney."

"That kid's a pain," Andrew said. "Always bugging me to go bicycle riding and stuff."

"He's a pain all right," Andy agreed. But it sounded disloyal to Briney even as he said it. You didn't take sides against your own brother. But… "Same time tomorrow," he said and switched off. Briney was thumping on the front door now.

"Hey, Andy, did you see my bike?" he asked as soon as Andy opened up. "I left it outside and it's gone."

"Did you lock it?"

"No. But it was in our own front yard," Briney wailed.

Andy walked ahead of him to the kitchen, opened the refrigerator and peanut-buttered a pickle. He let Briney rush to the back of the house to check the patio. He let him call next door to ask Jeff. He let him pick up the phone to call their father before he said, "Did you look behind the shrubbery at the side?"

Briney stopped dialing. "You put it there. You knew all the time."

Andy took an unconcerned bite. "I did it to teach you a lesson. Why don't you lock it and put it away? I always lock mine."

Briney's face was scarlet as he swung up his bag of newspapers. "You think you're so great. You're a pain, that's what. And who made you my mother? Who asked you to teach me lessons?" He slammed the door behind him.

Boy, is he mad! Andy thought. He grinned. And he thinks I'm the pain! He turned on the TV and sat down with his peanut pickle. Fighting with Briney had been good. It had kept the other thoughts from his head. He half-listened to a familiar TV commercial. An airplane droned overhead. Breaking the space-time continuum indeed! Andrew had to be kidding. But it probably would start raining tomorrow. And the game would be off. Everything had worked that way so far.

Jim Harrison didn't believe him next day though. "You're not copping out on me, are you Jordan?" he asked.

"No. Honest. The game will be rained out." He tried to make his voice sound certain, but it wasn't easy, standing out in the schoolyard under the clear blue of the sky.

"Well, it better," Jim Harrison said.

At lunch Andy sat down next to Gilbert in the cafeteria.

"I told you the way it would be," Gilbert said. "Jim Harrison was taking bets all morning that there'd be no game. It looked like he was getting plenty of takers." He looked hopefully at Andy. "Were you putting one over on him?"

"No," Andy said. "I think it *will* rain."

"Then that guy will for sure be a millionaire."

It was during last period that the rain started. Andy looked up from his math book, as stunned as anyone at the sound of the first drops hitting the window glass. It was weird all right because the sky wasn't even dark.

"Someone's turned a sprinkler on the window," Miss Carson said. She went across to look. "For heaven's sake. It's raining."

Gilbert looked reproachfully at Andy.

"I can't help it," Andy said. He felt his heart begin to pound. The deluge had begun.

He and Gilbert ran home, holding their books over their heads. Andy jumped his

21

hedge, skidding in mud that had already formed. Man! It was heavy rain.

Briney's bike was parked in the living room and he almost fell over it getting to the ringing telephone.

"Hello?"

"Andy. It's Jim Harrison."

Andy pushed one squelchy tennis shoe off with the toe of the other one.

Jim's voice was electric with excitement. "This is terrific, Andy. Do you know what we've got here? A goldmine."

"Yeah?" Andy could hear his heart begin to pound again. He wondered if a guy could get heart trouble this young.

"First off, tomorrow's Saturday. We'll go to the racetrack. You can study the horses and do your thinking tonight. We'll clean up."

"My parents like us to do stuff with them on the weekends," Andy said weakly. "Besides. It may be still raining."

"Naw. It won't last. My Dad lets me have the car on Saturdays so I'll pick you up."

"I don't think we'll be able to get into the track," Andy said. "I think there's an age level for gambling."

"We'll get in. You leave that to me. You go study the horses. Oh, I almost forgot. I'm having a party here at my house tomorrow night. You're invited."

Andy stared at his wet socks. One of Jim Harrison's all-time great parties and he was invited. Andy Klutz Jordan who hadn't been to a single party in the two years he'd been at Macmillan. Except Gilbert's birthday party. And that had been just the two of them and their families. He wished he had the nerve to ask if Betsy Hagan would be there. But that much nerve he'd never have. "Can Gilbert come?"

"Who?"

"Gilbert Spencer."

"Sure. Bring all your friends."

That wouldn't be hard, Andy thought as he put the phone down. Me and Gilbert. Gilbert and me. And even Gilbert hadn't been too friendly the last couple of days.

I think we should quit.
If there's any chance that
it could be us...

He could hear Briney's radio playing in his room so he knew the coast was clear to contact Andrew.

The red waiting light was on.

"It's still raining," Andrew told Andy. "Two people are missing in a flash flood."

Andy nibbled at his nails. Two people missing!

"Has it started there yet?" Andrew asked.

"Yes." Unconsciously Andy glanced out the window. "What about the dam?"

"It's still holding. But Andy, honest, I think we should quit. If there's any chance that it could be us...."

Andy thought about Jim Harrison's

party. "Let's keep going over the weekend anyway," he said. "That'll give it a chance to stop without us."

"Something else has happened, hasn't it?" Andrew asked.

No kidding, this guy knew him inside out. Andy told him first about the racetrack.

Andrew's eyes widened. "Man, that's cheating to say the least. It's probably even stealing."

"So? The racing business is full of cheats and thieves. But usually it's them stealing from the customers."

"I'm not going to tell you," Andrew said.

"Then we don't go to the party. Jim Harrison's giving it tomorrow night. All the song girls will be there. Betsy Hagan. All of them. I'll

25

tell you all about it. It'll be almost as good as being there yourself."

It was his trump card. He knew how hopelessly Andrew ogled the song girls. He knew how he felt about Betsy Hagan. Man, did he know!

Andrew's eyes slid away. "Well, I'll have to go find the Sentinel," he muttered and Andy knew he had won.

"I'll be back in ten," he said cheerfully. Mom always stacked last week's papers in the garage. Andrew would have no trouble finding the right one.

Rain hammered on the window as he fixed himself a sandwich. No sweat. It would be good for the ground. California always needed rain. They'd be glad of it come fire season.

"Racing cancelled because of rain," Andrew told him when he went back up. "We should have known."

It was almost a relief. "Well, he can't blame me for the rain," Andy said. And he thought, rain won't cancel the party. That's safe anyway.

"The party's off too," Jim told him when he called. Andy listened to the silence on the line and tried to read between the words. Was the party really off? Or had Jim decided that since Klutzy Andy couldn't help him this week, the heck with him?

"Troy Hamill's having a real wingding next Saturday though," Jim added. "I'll see you get invited. From now on, I'm taking care of your social life. Oh, there are a few favors I'm going to want you to do for me next week. Nothing much. I'll talk to you Monday."

"Sure."

Andy listened to the empty buzzing when Jim hung up. Had he meant, first the favors, then the party? It sure had sounded that way.

As soon as his Mom and Dad and Briney went shopping after lunch he dialed in Andrew. But the screen stayed dark. He waited a half hour and gave up. Something must have come up. Maybe Andrew's mom was having a "More exercise, less junk food" talk with him, right there in his bedroom. He'd get him tomorrow. Andrew would be itching to hear about the party that he didn't know had been cancelled.

It was that night at dinner that Andy's

27

dad mentioned the dam again. "I just hope that thing can take it," he said. "I've never seen rain like this."

Andy felt his meat loaf sticking in his throat. What if it didn't stop at all?

As soon as he wakened the next morning he heard the gurgling of overflowing gutters outside the house. The headlines in the Los Angeles Times spoiled his Sunday morning pancakes. Heck, he thought, a guy could get thin at this rate! He could hardly wait for the afternoon to check out the rain on the other world with Andrew. But the televiewer stayed black however frantically he pushed the buttons.

On Monday he stayed out of Jim Harrison's way, sneaking off campus at lunch-time to rush home to try the televiewer, just in case. But there was only the blank screen, staring back at him.

The talk in school was of nothing but the rain. The playing fields were flooded. Water had seeped in to cover the floor of the cafeteria. New umbrellas dripped in all the hallways. The smell of wet clothing was everywhere. Andy could concentrate on nothing.

As soon as classes let out he ran home and straight to the magnascreen. Please, he thought, please. His hands trembled so much that they had trouble with the televiewer buttons. But on the third try he pressed the right ones. Nothing. Three days in a row and nothing.

He sat staring at the lifeless square feeling his skin prickle, feeling sickness cold in his stomach. Andrew would never just stop without giving him warning. He'd be crazy to know about the party and what happened. If he could be at the televiewer he would be there.

Andy got up and paced around his room. He was scared, scared to death. He peered out of the window at Dopple Dam. The rain soaked hill looked black and menacing. The dam was a beast, ready to spring. It can't be, he thought. I won't let myself think it. A hill of water didn't come down there, sweeping everything in front of it, swallowing everyone in its path.

It was their fault. His fault. Andrew had wanted to stop, but he'd conned him into going on. He'd really known all along that they were breaking a natural law. He hadn't wanted to believe it, that was all.

Poor Andrew. Poor Mom and Dad and Briney who had been alive on that other world until just a few days ago. He'd go to the Sentinel and tell them the whole story. Maybe there was still some way to stop the disaster here. But would they believe him? There was no mirror planet on his screen now. He had no proof that there ever had been.

Briney was in the living room. He had spread a bunch of newspapers on the rug and he was using a rag to wipe the rain from his bicycle. Andy stared at the back of his brother's head. Briney couldn't swim that well. And that crazy old bicycle! What was the use of polishing it now?

He asked his father at dinner what would happen if the dam burst.

"I don't think it will, Andy. They're keeping an eye on it."

"But Briney can hardly swim," Andy wailed. "We ought to at least buy some lifejackets." His mom got up quickly and hugged him. She smelled of carbon paper and typewriter ribbon.

Andy clung to her. He clung to her again in the night when he wakened and thought he heard the wall of water rushing down the hill.

After she'd talked to him and told him it was only a dream, he lay, staring around his room. His books; the raggedy pennant on the wall; his beat-up work table. All of it special. The tele-viewer mocked him. All of it risked to get in good with Jim Harrison. To be special. From somewhere he seemed to hear Gilbert saying. "I thought you were special before." And he might have lost Gilbert's friendship too. But that didn't matter either. The deluge would wipe out all mistakes.

Tomorrow, he decided, he'd call the governor, and write to the Sentinel, and chalk warnings about the dam on all the walls and sidewalks. But there was such an inevitable feeling now about what was going to happen. He didn't know if anything could change it.

Sometime in the early hours of morning he slept and he wak-ened to his mother calling him for school. And to something else. The light on the televiewer was blinking! He lay, looking at it, disbelieving. Then he leaped out of bed and pushed the code buttons.

Andrew's face flickered on to the magnascreen. Behind him Andy could see his bedroom; the splotched desk, the raggedy pennant.

"Hi," Andrew said. "I thought I'd try to get you before you left for school."

"Where were you?" Andy asked faintly.

Andrew's knowing eyes looked into his. "Scared you, huh?"

"You don't mean you stayed away to …to scare me?"

"No. We had a power failure because of the rain. And then we were evacuated down to the school. Because of the danger from the dam. But I knew what you would be thinking." There was a smug satisfaction in Andrew's voice. "I figured it would teach you a lesson."

"Why you..! You were just as anxious to keep going as I was. Almost," he added, to be fair. "And who asked you to be my mother? Who asked you to teach me lessons?" He wanted to punch Andrew out. But the words had a familiar echo and he remembered where he'd heard

them before. Another one for the notebook. "Did the dam hold?" he asked weakly.

"Yes. Because the rain stopped on the day of the power failure. The day we quit talking to each other."

"Oh." Andy looked at his mirror image. "Well, that's it. We can't talk anymore. Anyway, we're special enough. Everything is." He felt light headed with relief.

"What are you jabbering about? Listen, I figure we could talk once in a while. Not enough to destroy the universe. Just enough to make life interesting."

"No." Andy put his hands on the wires. "Andrew, I've made a list of the things that bug me most about you. I'm going to study it. Maybe not having friends is our own faults. Maybe…"

Andrew interrupted. "I've made a list too. We think alike, remember? And you're pretty obnoxious yourself. But I guess you're OK a lot of the time too. I'm not real ashamed that you're me!"

They grinned at each other.

"Goodbye then, Andrew," Andy said and he grabbed all the wires on the televiewer and yanked them from the set.

In the silence he heard the rain lashing on the driveway. But it was OK. He knew it would stop. It was probably the last thing he'd ever know in advance. And he decided that that was OK too.

Maybe he'd just go down and make himself a sandwich for consolation...or to celebrate. Sandwiches were good for anything.

No, he'd invite Briney to go rain-cycling instead. Briney would like that. And Andy and Andrew could both use the excercise.

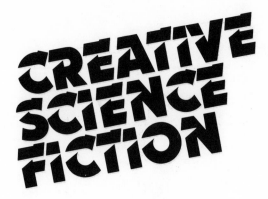

CREATIVE SCIENCE FICTION